Where the Magpie Meets Blue

By

Jiyoo Choi

Gold Moose Publishing books may be purchased for educational, business, or sales promotional uses. For information, please email us at hyeay@hyeay.com

ISBN: 978-1-969181-01-6

TABLE OF CONTENTS

Essays

Short Stories

About the Author **87**

Author's Note

I am an amalgamation of personalities. My parents raised me through nine moves, and I've sculpted myself into different versions everywhere, every time. I've made myself purposely malleable to fit into the frames of life in Illinois, New Jersey, Seoul, New Delhi, and Gurgaon—but who did I *want* to become? An introvert, ambivert, or an extrovert? Did I have autonomy in my personal adjustment, or was that choice too much to ask as a child, now a teenager, and almost a young adult?

In this work, I explored how various facets of my identity address my uncertainty. I extrapolated from the dichotomies that have shaped who I am: consistency and change, complacency and autonomy, ability and disability, and extroversion and introversion. Every so often, I've had downturns of turmoil in my sense of self and relationships and periods where I was surrounded by overwhelming positive influence. Every new home became another challenge to test my ability to change or even forge my identity, because the correct answer to the standardized test always required change in myself. My mom tells me that my greatest strength is my versatility, some of my friends see me as an artist, and other friends view me as a scientist; I expect myself to check all the

1

boxes because I've always seen myself subject to possibility and ambition. At the intersection, I reconciled with how I have and haven't met their expectations: will I be an extrovert with leadership, an ambivert with flexibility, and an introvert with calmness, all at the same time?

From my memories moving and readjusting as a child, I analyzed the cornerstones of how I've navigated changes in my physical space, through recollecting the tangible items, the ingredients of my life. These artifacts became my muses. The letters I've collected since I was a child, crochet yarn from middle school, and the books piled on my nightstand all served as inspiration and became part of the melting pot, which grew and boiled into a discussion of the future: I examined whether a future home in a bustling city would accept my introverted side, if I could let my ambiversion shine through like a dual narrative, and what doors of possibility had opened for my extroverted side to share my disability.

I wanted my project to be varied and complete like an actual exhibition that engages, evokes, and compels its audience. To question whether I was an introvert reader and writer, an ambivert artist and debater, or an extrovert advocate and daughter—or a true persona of interdisciplinary identity.

At times, I hope that everyone will see this project before they meet me, and sometimes I wonder if I never want to be vulnerable at all. Imagine these rooms not as conversations or unanswered questions hanging like hooked question marks, but as a complete exhibition in a corner of a museum. Each frosted white room decorated with poetry cast on walls and slides rolling through a warm beam from a luminescent projector. Art falling from the ceiling and headphones wired into my experience. A complete collection of my 17-year-old odyssey to explore the spectrum of introversion, ambiversion, and extroversion.

Poems

A Silver Moth

Somewhere in this house a moth lies dormant, asleep or
dead or somewhere in between. My mom said that it had shining
wings like silk, silver and rippling like turquoise waves, barely aflutter
and exhaling, beautiful and bounded.

I pry open the lock of my bedroom when I hear it's gone—first
sight of an insect feels like freshly cut nails grating my insides.

But I cupped ladybugs in my soft pink-veined
palms and pet young butterflies like they were
meant to be loved. I ran from larvae and poured
sweet breath over the caterpillars, pretty
paradoxes.

No moth crawled out of hiding for eerie flames. Maybe moth sounds
too close to mother and I feel sorry for the weak but beautiful
because they remind me of all those I've lost.

Somewhere under the weathered couch or the runner or in
the grooves of the windowsill, a moth lies in limbo.
I let it linger in peace.

Being a Collector

We speak in silent prayers, in the dark we
stumble into the big open, large gap in the canvas
we call home. Scratch backs until traces turn
ruddy and bright, children under the canopy
but adults hanging over the veranda verge.

Let's go where you avoid: past the garden,
through the obscured mirrors, over the picket
fence, digging your nails across the patchy white
woodwork, submerge your soul with
glasses as soiled goggles.

Pretend we'll stick together like the humid July air when
you fall apart like rain shrapnel. Pretend the life you've lived
is worth something greater than the modern poetry
that writes itself, lulling and dormant in some strange way. Pretend
you trust yourself to walk in a straight line and you can recite
the alphabet backwards and call home before the sun rises,

cold face and tired but so clear-minded. Pretend that you're scared
someone will understand this reference. Pretend you want
to be understood. Pretend you'll stop yourself from thrashing

around your fibrous body in the open after midnight. Pretend you
think writing is meaningful and confidence is something
you're used to like breathing. Pretend you breathe.

Pretend you don't count every breath you take. Pretend that you want
to be yourself sans fear of succumbing to an unknown standard,
all-knowing and ravenous for the souls of teenaged fury. Pretend
you still know who you want to become. Say your life isn't
like those who run around, stupid and boneless in the twilight. Say
you wake up to see the sunrise like the last time wasn't four years ago.
Say everything you want like no one's watching anyways.

Circuits

i.

An aphorism,

blue—like time under covers

concentrated into small capsules that scream when you crack them

dead and skull-less against the wailing walnut counter. Was it forever

you compressed in backpacks and ballpoint pens and love letters

or invitations to love through a mirrored mirage? Did you lose

some part of yourself to loathe your art? Did you kill somebody

to become who you are? God, am I allowed to be

a shell of my older self?

ii.

I think that the azure magpie is artful as it perches on gables

because it is a zephyr, spring into summer, slow ripple in water,

the rising heat of a star. I know the waves crash into caves where

some seagulls nest and steal from us for their hatchlings. I touch

the smooth gilt of the picture frame, because it reminds me of

stubborn floral remnants beneath my nails when I pulled dahlias

from the meadows. I weep when the slit in stem is so overtly

somber in the vase; I turn away from the oxalis glued to the sun.

A feeling when I learned to hate yourself is a sin.

iii.

Poetry is so difficult like asking mothers where their daughters

find peace when they breathe love into their own daughters. It seeps

through holes in ceilings when there are no words to describe

the inevitable circuit that lights new life and cuts out the old.

Every word hangs like a quiet question mark,

a mole that grounds roots under veins, silently rebels against

the subversion you wished to be her own.

Distilled Remembrance

You held the world in the face of your palms

Your palms—scale-like and cracked like aging earth

You ebbed like gentle seafoam in moonlight but now

You inhale tarnished sand and apologize for cold ash

You remember your braided veins and tight shoulders when

Your hollow cork bones exhale expired wine

But wine never expires, *does it?*

The scent of fermented ginkgo beans hangs from

Your collarbone, protruding like knuckles in stiff hands

A clay jeopshi, a dry bowl spun from leftovers and graywater

Your fingertips corrode baby backs with detergent

Smooth like April soil and unwelcome like mid-life storms

You sink like distilled air at dinner tables past ten

Ten past eight, hwahyejang ripped off rosy sandpaper feet

Your words tumble like old dimes asleep in threadbare pockets

Change always kept, never taken—for granted

You billow like decay and dust trapped in fading limelight

You wallow for the fate of a thousand dying stars

You pined for a sprouting future from wrinkled black figs

You clung to the last rays of summer sun

You blossomed in the Gardens of Babylon

Somber heart of an eldest daughter/mother, do you remember?

Flowers Grow from the Chemicals I Spattered

And maybe
You'll understand the feeling:

The ceiling sinks under the weight of the world,
Reeling in a place that drowns—finite, misunderstood
Because I feel too much and you turn me inside-out for
A dream that wavers like it's caught in a breeze
In a branch that was meant to be cut down, on some tree long
Gone. I think you pulled my shirt until it evolved into a dress
Like the geraniums that grow, wild and untethered

and reverie.

I've seen the Ge on my periodic table attach to flesh and
Gaps and the germanium smudges into geranium because
I yearn for a future in the boundless plains, more astounding
And great and fulfilling than the titrations and erlenmeyer flask
And stirring rods that sit impatiently
For me to rebut their fragility.

Food, korea, paraphernalia

The balance, rustic, yellowed, creaking under
the weight of two suns: one sweltering and exhausted
like the collapse of a trying star, one wine-soaked,
broiling, bathing in a brilliant, gilded birth, proud
in the face of bulging doubt. You held a warmth
like a timeless August sun and oven-nestled sourdough
in a cherry wood kitchen. Pickled yuzu-honey radish
on slow-cooked white rice and red bean bingsoo
bulging with frosted milk flakes inside sun-stained
bronze bowl. Somber sweet summer showers blessed
each bone in spine and sunset picnic paraphernalia
wrapped into uncanned peach jars. Wailing at the sight of a
bejeweled bruise the color jujube, burnt, smoldered
porcelain in wayward heels, gleam of unused silver chopsticks
perched on heart of mother.

Ghazal for Universal Introversion

In a corner, I stare moon-eyed. A seed of vastness as I deflect the
universe. A satellite hangs above. I swirl barley seeds in

my mouth like coins I cannot swallow: a head, a tail. A tail, two heads.
This vessel was carved to fit the roof of my mouth. I curl within

a corner, like fate sculpted to be inside. In this room, mother stitches
color to curtains and warmth to broth, boiling until stove is a basin

molded for barley tea, like it was fashioned to take up
space—spluttering onto the kitchen floorboards, coaxing each splinter
into thread, chagrin

into herbal delight. An eldest daughter is her mother's sun, yet an
only child is her mother's sleepless nights: an implosion of her
universe when I refrain

from the world, collapsed stars into supernovas when I am an opaque
mirror of her doing, a cataclysm of fruitless seeds when I lull parched
and thin.

I deflect because I cannot reflect my mother. The coins tumble like
decades of regret, lost "what-ifs" spiraling into oblivion. God knows

what lurks in the coffin

unless I peel it open. The world is a knife or a star or a double-edged
sword, who knows? In the cupboards, pockets of yuzu tea carpet the
milky sheepskin

from which a tail, a head extends–it cranes its neck towards the
whisper of light from two adamant doors. Moonlight, sunlight,
serenity or din.

I hang like an unanswered question, as if I could stretch like the
galaxy, hoping it never rips apart. In this universe, I cradle this fear,
thickened margin

between daughter and mother. When life swells with impossible
breadth, she tells herself that her daughter will stir like the sunrise.
Light will glisten on her chin

raised above the horizon. She will inherit her mother's overt
resilience, her need to break the earth's core and fasten it together,
underpin

all scarred pieces. She will quench the stars and lick tassels
of radiance. She will fluoresce, vibrant and clean of sin

and guttering dust. I sink teeth into tongue, tender jujube in core of flesh. I am no sunrise daughter but a still mannequin

as my mouth grows numb. Metallic sweetness subdues soft tea. For now, it lingers in the back of my throat. For now, stinging aftertaste and sun are akin.

guilt inherited

your guts don't feel like they're falling apart.
some feel like they've turned into boulders,
the hardest, roughest, jagged, and serrated river bedrocks,
ambushed by currents inside you. some others,
the skipping stones, bloat and float upwards,
skimming up your esophagus.

your appendix warps into a pebble,
your pancreas—a slab of gravel.
a tsunami of skipping stones bottled in your throat.

you remember the stones were once a pagoda.
somewhere, pebble stacks fulfill wishes,
but you stood under your too-tall wishing tower,
a skyscraper of shelved dreams.
it tips over and smites you in a thousand different places—
a thousand in cacophony.

the stones fall into limbo
between heaven and hell, or heaven and earth?

half-bloom

wounded from the womb, peonies
bloom where scratches are sewn.
i dig pits into skin where bulbs erupt—
bulbs of baby blue hydrangeas seared
crimson. what is beauty without pain?
i dunk the bouquet into the toilet. a hurricane of
petals & fertile bile flush. face flushed, i whispered
do you love me whole? i'll crush seeds
in your kitchen, pluck you unripe,
plant you six feet under. mother,
this won't be a light harvest. flowering
season starts in may, in vain. rose stems
like asparagus. diced on the cutting board,
these wounds are freshly picked. 50% off
at the drugstore because everything's better
cheaper: cheaper polyester, cheaper confessions,
cheaper paper rings, cheaper tulips
on clearance. collecting dust,
I'll walk the aisle alone. i'm free
to take but you'll pay to play. bury hyacinths for free
flowers forever. burn this bush before i sprout
as bloodsucking termites. lead me on &
i'll lead you to the woods.

I

don't know
what to tell you at the edge of the garden,
hands-cross linked and vision blurred, enough—
I think the magpie sits on this rooftop
haven because everything that lurks under feels pretty
unexplainable and wavering like the small purple laced
under your eyes, permanent and streaked and crocheted
to the ivory fiber of the orange peel astray on the sidewalk.

I'm scared that this is too beautiful
to stay alive. I'm scared that I'll scare you away from
exploring all the beautiful places I was too scared of.
I'm scared that the things I claimed were sacred tokens,
untouchable and best left locked on the glass shelf, were
lost stars that died without a chance to explode into something
beautiful.

In Light of Rigoberta Menchú Tum

Branches extend into the heavens,
roots wrap and sprawl across the underworld—

The earth is forgiving.
worshiped for ever-lasting divinity as it is scorched

Under the rays of the cruel, pulsing sun
a provider who gifts this grueling life.

have I let the fire ignite my skin ablaze? it barely scratched me as I
glared, relentlessly smote the burgundy land

swallowed by the seductive forces of ambition, I
swallowed the triumph that pillows on the walls of

my esophagus. it rests without a fight, nestled, cuddled in my throat
like a pacified baby, rocking back and forth until I forget

and remember that sweet, filling aftertaste of humility.
a suppressant that relieves sins and artifices

sought to replace me and everyone before me. forgiven,
I return to the barren land where that pulsing heart

strips my indulgence, floods my own heart,

& I engrave insignias of blood to remind myself

I am not alone; somebody is watching.

but what now usurps the potency of this burning heart?

neither an outstretched hand with fingertips yearning with ardor, nor

zealous, blazing breaths gone berserk.

the earth felt a metallic aftertaste of blood in its mouth when you

impaled its gums, strangling its throat with a cocked gun to its head

and you struck–

you scorched the earth until it burst into a thousand shards, spears

impaled and blood snaked

into a grasp that quenched the beat of that burning heart, and it

rotted under the shroud they used to veil its cold ash.

I was stuck in this limbo between heaven and earth and hell but you

parched purgatory until its burnt edges curled into the abyss.

this force pulled all of us to the end of the world, and we saw the

world ending before you slit our eyes and shoved sound into the pit

of our stomachs. through the esophagus that once nested humility,

you bore serrated terror.

Kissed

limbo and limerence and liminal spaces

lime and light and dark and sunset

leaves and shadows and glistening midnight puddles

around yellowing lampshade with scratches

decay and dust next to a bell and a suncatcher

hanging from the glass door of the convenience store

the light hits the suncatcher in all its beautiful places

It tucks into the crevices and curves and weaves, subtle enough

to be perfume bottle with a rose tint and with the last of rose
fragrance

but ravenous like starved sparrow hatchlings

a subdued atmosphere with light through white curtains

and slow clock ticking and home and homeliness and a breeze

and reliance and responsibility sitting on the wooden floor

silhouettes of the darkened wooden chairs and the light

passing thru the legs of the chairs like a chess board

and the light reaching my book and my fingers

the light is reverie

the light shines above

the light is a muse

the light passes us

my mom on my shoulder and my neck on the windowsill

cold droplets of relief on forehead and a realization

that my back was meant to be blessed

by the ephemeral kiss of sun,

a caring and resilient daughter

Life, Rated

Perhaps if you rated my life based on how much

I've lived, you would pause the screen and

touch the delicate skin of the universe, soft underarm

steamed in 들기름 and all the flavors repugnant to white

man's tongue, and scroll through the comments to search for

what would be a sufficient answer: the nights I fell asleep

in knotted ponytails and sweat-baked makeup, the 3 am

odysseys I typed, nails against platform like runaway heels,

the mornings where I woke up sweaty and estranged.

White Silverado enters the garage, bulked and bulging

with electrolytes and cold plunges—enough

to fuel the engine for the half-marathon you'll run

in an attempt to escape from sweaty corporate desolation.

Pilates lesson in five, Nissan Altima spurs in three,

three point five stars for *How would you rate Jesse's service?*

Do you know what these plastic pixel decimals entail

despite that every word is not a knife or a double-edged sword

or a Hanja letter obscured by the dark of your own doing?

Wrinkled pages flitter in workbook like a storm for your own good,

each step in the wooden hallway, a clue to whose curious finger

dares to twist the knob, empty Gatorade sinks in the corner

where you've abandoned dreams incited with instant coffee packets.

caffeinated fiber of the country exhausted and excited and catalyzed to be in full cycle, full-circle, fulfilled and whole and enough

knotted in some chaos of 야근 and karaoke nights that you never cared enough about, cared enough about motivation and stimulation *enough crying,* enough emotion, enough han in the roots of ancestral tree.

run girl run

And you spout

Boisterous truths that lay sprawled on the desk, soulless

Condescension laced like you want me to overdose and

Die. I think if you swallowed down the words you thought were

Enough to impress, you'd look more like a person, like you knew

Four-fifths of what you were doing. You just reek of

Grandiose lies spewed instead of real thoughts found in the

Heat of the moment. Can you gauge your heart open? I wonder

If you knew what I was thinking you'd screw

Jars and gears in your jaws until your cheeks grow sullen and you hurl

Knee-deep in salt water. Cleanse your mouth until the cavities from

Lackluster lust expels itself from your rancid breath. Crawl

Mourning the time you spent hating. Bet you'll confuse

Numbness for healing as you run, foot in wet concrete, step all over

Open wounds, screeching and yelling, reeling tires, stumble over

Pulsing like you'll feel less alone at the end of this marathon.

Quiver like a butterfly at the edge of the railing like wings akimbo like

Running isn't enough like they point when you can't run like a girl.

Sons will tell you trinity is truth & beauty & goodness but you

Tread to even reach one. They say breaststroke or backstroke or get

Under but now you look stupid being beautiful, naive yet aware yet

Vexed in false positives in red lines, red herrings, red—*too much*—

What snakes around your arm and into veins is not what you wanted.

Xenon anesthesia rivals biking across bridges at sundown,

Yearning for some alternative to fluking this act that your

Zeal is dying for.

sixteen is entropy

at the edge of the universe, a star dies & a nebula is born.
in celebration, the universe birthed flame to sixteen

fuchsia candles that erupted into a storm
full of wildfire, charring skin & comets & my heart.

I parch my pillowcase with bloodshot eyes, pulsing, burning,
yearning. ravenous as I bite the flesh of my conscience,

pull near the edge of the abyss, never look back, & drown
the pounding in my head. hours ago, i turned sixteen.

the death of a thousand stars seared my insides, scorching
hundreds of wishes that hung in a lost lump, limp like a second

heart. i wrestle my sheets, hide from moonlight & the luster of chaos,
the universe. in a heartbeat, my guts churn into a whirring chaos,

entropy. nature always returns to a chaotic state, pulsing moonlight
running in veins, running from that nauseating vision of you

& your prophecies & you. in a heartbeat, you'd run
from me to Stanford & Silicon Valley, heart beating for success

light-years away. will you die scintillating & beloved, triumphant
in the face of every child-prodigy-burnout or burn out

like a dying star, spitting fumes of planetary feces in my face?
will you prove the Riemann hypothesis

or will you look back, mourning that you peaked in high school?
have you crumpled up in the face of your education?

educating you to write between fine lines, suffocate in neat rows,
teaching me to cover up & sit straight.

covered up in rayon & hair compressed so straight
it pierces beneath my clothes where there's no flesh underneath.

 a pig, an extraterrestrial with lipstick, hoping i pulverize
 as i launch into the atmosphere. in nature, entropy always increases

over time: the only constant is change. my childhood is a fleeting,
slipping facade, a churning, glittering, pulsing chaos of every second,

every heartbeat loose in perpetuity– sixteen.

Sunset Regrets (after "Mirror" by Rita Dove)

Mirror

Hold you within

Palms cracked

Will sunken, incandescence dull.

Arrows like bent ribs

Against

Thousands of estranged letters.

Learn to forget

Lost gazes,

Remembrance brittle,

Fracturing like

Demeanor of glass.

Heartstrings ripped like loose threads,

Eyebags perennial, stubborn like echoes.

Find sunsets,

Meaningless evenings, and silver.

Reflection—now past.

I am enough.

Mirror,

Within you hold

Cracked palms

Dull incandescence, sunken will.

Ribs bent like arrows

Against

Letters estranged of thousands

Forget to learn

Gazes lost,

Brittle remembrance,

Like fracturing

Glass of demeanor.

Threads loose like ripped heartstrings,

Echoes like stubborn, perennial eyebags.

Sunsets find

Silver and evenings meaningless.

Past—now reflection.

Enough, am I?

The Apple

The subway screeches to a stop for a stampede tilted
along the rush hour platform—crowds eclipse
the horizon until the asphalt is blonde and corporate.

Buzz and hustle are at core of this city: if I bit into the
apple its seeds would burst into cacophony. Manhattan is
all but a haven for introversion.

I stretch from Soho to Greenwich like a shadow
at the break of dawn. A harrowing echo underneath
where wheels pull silhouettes into strings,

mirages spring from seared concrete, charred scales
against Earth. Vibrant signs hang from oak, half-read
newspaper on a bench. A blue Citi Bike halts and glides

into wavering plains, a green square in the center
of steel and skyscrapers—I watch streetlights fuse into pine
and furnish this infinite room,

witness sunlight unfurl in curtains of willow,

catch a sparrow in a stalemate with a neighboring
squirrel. Heartfelt handshake under a gate

near 8th Avenue as paint blossoms under a leafy
stroke. In Central Park, I find an opening for solitude.
An introvert survives in the heart of urban chaos.

you held the world

you held the world in the face of your palms—scale-like, aging earth,
gentle seafoam in moonlight: apologies in unfurled fingers

braiding calloused veins like my mother's third grade hair. your bones
iron under the weight of war but now hollow cork against dementia.

remember? you, a fledgling torn from home, saw the steel boat of a
thousand displaced souls erupt from an incendiary seed

while mother looked back, knuckles protruding from a stiff
grasp, faltering like a dead dry bowl in the kiln. when your feet tied

themselves to southern shorelines, you watched them corrode, ignite
the mountains with pumped fists. when all you had left were

two clay jeopshis and a first name—no family to share your last—you
crushed tear-stained seaglass until your smile lines weren't the only

cracks: something you shared, at last. now, the sun sways limp in the
sky, like the fall scent of fermented ginkgo hanging from

your collarbone. you billow like decay and dust
trapped in fading starlight, or rather, the hospital

light that your breath clings to, the last rays of summer sun—

just before they killed summer, you were the youth of june.

Tired

in a boundless grid of led lights and vessels of electricity, a child sits
wide-eyed, clouded vision with a mirage of hot tears that pool
on a desk where papers fall like a monsoon that never ends.

장마 is a reiteration of the tale of 웅녀—a desperate bear who
starved in a cave, subsisting on onions until she became human. act
of discipline close to self harm than dedication. a tribute to prove

nothing to herself but that pain worth burying nails into flesh & sod
had paid off in forms only she understood. God, it is so tiring
to swim in a pond when the rain won't end

where rain turns into droplets of sapphire. Sharp corners like edge
of knife, tearing umbrellas and open palms because what is
a world with reward without pain? You turn your hands upside

down and flat. Let diamond marbles and rubies pool
in a puddle under the wooden desk, no yearning, no want.
The city grows wheels and reels, screams, takes flight,

crashing down like the waves adjacent to the horizon, running
to *get better*, yelling to walk two steps ahead, checking

as if there's no time and you'd rather fall down the stairs

than lose the race as the bell rings, as the clock ticks.
The stars didn't hang in the sky since the beginning of time,
someone with nail and hammer in hand and enough determination

made what you couldn't. The green-blue under your fingernails
is stubborn like guilt you feel for loving yourself instead of grating
away your skin and bones and youth for something greater.

Your birthday was embedded in my email address

I don't care enough
to tell you   why   flocks of sparrows
have survived in the traffic-jammed,   sweltering asphalt
but scurry off   December pine trees.

I pretend   I don't see
tear-stained galaxies   bloom from the job
you never cared less about
but just cared enough
to never quit.

I don't care when   you weave the truth
into a tilted lie   when I want   the unabridged sentence.
I cover your face
with a camera glare
behind your birthday picture.

I don't care if you cry on your seventeenth.
I don't care if you sit in teenaged fury.
I don't care if you gauge out your hippocampus
& erase my face on purpose.

I don't answer when you ask to use the rest of the
Swiss souvenirs that sat in a sad slump on my desk.

I don't care if they're used.
I don't care if you take flight.
I don't care if you replace the old.
I don't care, enough.

Essays

For Granted

I have this habit of procrastinating until I finish a piece of hard candy from my drawer. Nowadays, I just bite into it instead; if all is inevitable and my time, my youth, as a student, a teenager, a daughter, and a friend, is fleeting, I would rather embrace the imminence than avoid it.

I was an ambitious, anxious child. I wanted to be an indispensable part of society, and I believed that I could achieve anything with sufficient effort. My education was a stepping stone to broader accomplishments, and although I was often interested in the content I was learning, I felt more invested in my progress as a student.

To find joy in learning, in cultivating knowledge, in the process of acquiring a worldview, I had to learn to appreciate the process itself. It is a known fact that education is a privilege, and I did value my opportunities, but I didn't understand the implications of what I could do with my education. I was bored, disappointed with the seemingly rigid confines of my knowledge. Hence, I took my opportunities for granted, isolating my time, the insight I garnered from the classroom from my life outside of school.

I always felt like the abstract concepts I learned in school never had practical applications to my life. I've always loathed the feeling that what I've learned may not contribute to my future career. But if I'm going to be a high school student for the next two years, an undergrad for the next four, and, most likely, a graduate student, I would rather embrace my role. I experienced a paradigm shift this summer. Thanks to the help of many others, I feel like there are less boundaries to what I can accomplish with my education. I feel like I can harness the power I have as a student, the agency to ask questions, be curious, and not be judged by others older than me. Even if I don't know something, no one will judge my lack of knowledge because I'm not supposed to know everything yet. For now, I love what it means to be a student.

Go Gina

Last spring, my English teacher consigned me with her class for a couple minutes. She said that she trusted me most out of all the people in the room - including some upperclassmen who were four years older than me. That wasn't new news. Teachers tend to believe I'm reliable; I look the part, at least. Glasses, straight hair, gets along with most people: I'm the epitome of your average eldest-Asian-immigrant daughter. I don't do anything that seems unreasonable, and that's why she told me I was a "forty-year-old woman in a fourteen-year old's body," and that's why she thought I was literally more mature than her, a millennial in her late twenties. To fourteen-year-old me, that was a benign compliment. Now, that concerns me. I stayed up one night last year, scrambling to finish a paper that was due that morning. I wondered where it all went wrong, where life began to feel debilitating. I've always attributed my mishaps to my greatest, insurmountable weakness, my lack of motivation, but throughout these past few months, I've realized there are a myriad of inherent causes behind my hollow desires. Take this interview from a year ago, for instance:

Interviewer: Let's get started. What do you consider your greatest strength?

Me: I strive for perfection, and I'm always ready to put in my full effort. I'm also really motivated when it comes to my passions and extracurriculars, but I think my greatest strength is definitely my flexibility and tolerance towards unexpected hardships, for example, when I participated in...

My inner monologue that haunts me during intense social situations: I am somewhat a perfectionist, but since nothing can be done perfectly, I'm easily disillusioned from my goals. And because I'm a perfectionist, if I fail, I try to "fake it 'til I make it," or I pretend that I can take on more responsibilities until I disintegrate. That's why I appear tolerant and accepting towards hardships. To balance out all this disillusionment, I constantly need new, shallow inspiration to fuel my short-lived aspirations, and when I can't find those -

Interviewer: That's great, I love how you overcame that in your community. Hey um, might be hard to tell me as an interviewee, but what do you think is your weakness?

Me: uhh, probably taking on too many responsibilities, even when I feel pressured. I've been improving on this, though, last week I...

My inner monologue: clearly a bit more authenticity here, but unless I express this out loud, no one seems to notice that I feel pressured. That's what concerns me. Even though I feel suffocated by my responsibilities, I'm a virtuoso, an Oscar-winning actress, when it comes to pretending like I can afford a couple more assignments or duties on my to-do list. My English teacher's testimony proves it all: my spurious approach to life fools the eyes of others. The reason I've had so much difficulty changing is because I don't feel the need to. Other people perceive me as more grounded than I actually am. I tend to be extreme, especially with my concept of discipline. I've held on to this morphed definition of sustainability - not spending, going out, or doing anything new. I stayed at home working and living in my own bubble and thought that was how it was supposed to be for me (someone told me I was living like a reclusive monk) and I was afraid of feeling the guilt of indulgence through consuming new things - and that guilt felt harrowing and haunting. All that "discipline" collapsed one day, even when it had never come to fruition in the first place.

My guilt of self-indulgence, more like self-tolerance, ties into the uptight paranoia of Gina, the character, or Sza's nervous persona in her song Go Gina; hence the title, go gina! Similar to Sza's life at college, I'm at a place where my lifestyle is forced to be different, and I'm trying new things, but now I don't know if I'm losing the groundedness that I once had; what I've been slightly evading is that I don't know if I'm getting out of my comfort zone, or if I'm trying to become someone I'm not. I've moved to a large city from the almost rural New Jersey suburbs, joined groups of people I wouldn't have been interested in three months ago, and found myself truly "living" according to other people's standards. In her new friend group, Sza doesn't know "who [she] can trust," in the same way that I feel distant from the new types of people I'm meeting, and certain personal conflicts have reduced parts of my trust in people. On the surface, my life seems more intriguing than before, but sometimes it feels superficial and intractable. Managing this new identity crisis along with constant, inevitable change just seems futile at times, but maybe this is the process of growing.

My sense of self wavers like Sza's, because our old selves "bring [us] out of character" and anchor us back into our uptight apprehension. Go Gina is a song dedicated to cheer up our inner Gina, to remind our anxious self that even when things feel out of control, even when we're the ones making these decisions. Rather than repressing Gina and ignoring her existence entirely, the idea of fulfilling and acknowledging her needs maintains my peace.

Because I've learned how to accept and balance these sudden changes, I feel ready to embrace how others have perceived me. I've grown and matured, so I feel internally aligned with my grounded external persona. I relate to Go Gina so much because I'm trying in the same way that Sza is trying,

trying to let go, trying to learn, and trying to make room for both growth and Gina.

It's slightly terrifying to reveal this level of vulnerability, but it's also terrifying to imagine a future where I can't improve because I can't embrace vulnerability. This is my best for now; I tried.

Ihae-hada: To Understand

When I was younger, I traced the golden outlines of the necklaces around my mother's neck, searching for an unabridged sense of the world within the crevices of the linked chains. I stuck my pinky finger into the corners of a buckled car seat, pointed at all the signs in the hallways, peered into the doorlock on my knees, pulled each fiber of the edge of ripped construction paper, and colored my world with the paint of the words I found on the streets. I felt this inherent desire, creeping up my esophagus, asking to define every part of the universe I wanted. I felt this unknown necessity to proclaim that I needed to know everything, see everything, learn everything, and do everything—not out of greed or motivation or success, but to feel everything, to understand what it is to be complete. I am a mosaic of not everything I've loved, but all that I've loved and loathed, because I would be a miniature puzzle and not the Michaelangelo-sized mural that I wanted to become. I was born with the desire to ihae.

In Finding Heung

After I turned six months old, I spent my early life in Schaumburg, Illinois, visiting nearby colleges as the only regional monuments, basking in the corn fields that plagued the midwest. But unlike the corn husks that lay akimbo and haphazardly across the dry sod of Chicago outskirts, my parents refused to settle in the tranquility of the boundless plains—the world was vast, stretching afar and beyond seas of unripe ivory corn. My parents were like corn grains; we were adaptable; we were miniscule; we were infinitely possible because we could migrate to wherever sans the fear of leaving too much behind. We never left behind much, and I felt grateful in the smallness of my life compared to the sense of possibility of the world, freedom and unbounded joy in the hope of a new place.

The nature of transience embedded in my life rejected all sorrow of departure. My mom used to read me vibrant picture books, stories of bunnies and llamas and small animals with strangely human lives. When she'd fall asleep on her side, I'd pretend the space created by her arched legs were my castle, and I was the puppy princess, inextricably glued to the tales inside my tower and the soft purple linen of my mom's pajamas. My eyes never shut as long as a book cuddled open in my arms. And because these western happy books cheered my early upbringing into a sunshine paradise, I was a happy American child, who just happened to love reading. Until I moved to Korea, I never felt the desperation that brimmed in the Korean folk tales of the iconic tortoise and hare, the fear of sacrifice in the tale of *Gyeonwoo and Jiknyeo*, or even the exasperating responsibility in the story of *Shimchong*. I never related to strong emotion; the concept of unexplainable guilt felt too intense, churning, burning, tethered and heavy.

My first memory of identity was when I was five years old, digging my nails into the turf that surrounded the kindergarten playground. I clutched an empty pink lunchbox, bejeweled with stickers of Disney characters plastered across the stainless-steel surface, which once held a delicacy of steamed mandu, or Korean dumplings. Despite the narrowness of my eyes, the English laced with my mom's Korean accent, and the excitement that brewed in the basement of my Korean Saturday school, learning taekwondo forms of *poomsae* to Kpop songs, I was none but American. There was no dichotomy to be dealt with; I could be whoever I wanted. The scattered hopscotch and the shallow end of the pool and the ballet studio and rainbow loom charm bracelets were where I sought freedom—but, most importantly, I was American in fantasies of knowledge flashcards and piles of chapter books.

My ability to read soon became inextricably linked with my persona. I resided in the Edgewater Public Library; I ensured every monthly payment was my parents' money's worth by flitting through the pages of books as the facility shut down. I grappled with both quality and quantity, a novel agape in my lap, feeding my reading list as much as I could within limited library working hours. In the divots of time that I didn't sulk over tragedies or venture through Harry Potter and Magic Tree House series, I pondered what I would recreate as a writer, poet, storyteller, learning and writing, exploring and weaving, free.

And so a writer was who I was, with dreams of soaring freely into the brilliant American azure, not a single cloud in sight—until I moved to dust-blue skied Korea. My Korean peers praised my English, ability to consume books at higher lexiles like I was ravenous, each stickered spine adding to the shelf, flawless journal entries, and pristine American clothes from J. Crew. I earned tassels, medals, paraphernalia meant to reward something I loved when it was a game for everyone but me. Inundated with the perception that English was a skill meant to be refined and polished, I was no longer left to grow sun-soaked in the wilderness. By the time I entered second grade, I had exhausted all my energy in improving my Korean spelling skills in 받아쓰기, conjugating verbs into polite forms, practicing the kpop dances, and collecting cute but utterly useless paraphernalia from the stationary store, drawing my friends as anime characters: the American girl who aspired to be an author now dreamed of such a Korean future.

Running my hands across the crisp spines stuck in my bookshelf, I felt guilt and some unfiltered anger that I had burned out, given up, lost potential to mindlessly succumb to the Korean standard. Did I lose my identity? Could I still astonish others with my writing and reading? Was I even proficient for my age anymore? Where was the girl who strived to go above and beyond, the desire to love and inspire in her eyes? As I anxiously guessed, intuitive clicks on the reading comprehension test, each question flickered by like the possibility of a better future. My mom told me that I scored higher than most of my age group on the test, but I didn't feel enough. I could've done better, read further, accomplished *greater*. Was it even worth trying when every attempt felt like a debilitating bullet to my identity? What did this reveal about myself? Was I the type to give up when I didn't understand, when I couldn't acknowledge? I didn't know. I sat tethered and hot and heavy and tainted.

When I moved to India and enrolled in the American Embassy School in New Delhi, I was glad to start over, but unhappily went through the process of recognizing the manslaughter I'd committed to my English. I dug my fingernails into my fleshy palms when the English entrance exam I'd hoped to be a reading comprehension quiz was a speaking test. The teacher, patient but indifferent, pointed to an illustration of a family of bears inside a kitchen: one grabbing honey out of a magenta cabinet ajar, one coloring with crayons in the corner of a suave, navy dining table, one gazing into a handheld mirror, next to curtains the shade of coral, windowsills toned walnut-wood. I sheepishly muttered that there were three bears. What else was I supposed to say?

Confused and startled, I peered at her indifferent expression, a face of *I knew this would happen*—I looked down at the fleece carpet. I wanted to tell her that the bears lived in a strange house painted with *awkward* colors, that the crayons were too big for the small bear who was too stupid to know what he was drawing, that bear was *unhygienic*, grabbing honey with its bare paws, that the bears were *individualistic*, that I knew the meaning of *fatigued* and it was exactly how I felt, but not what I was saying. But her indifference told me it wouldn't matter whether I knew all these words because it would never be enough. My words, my interrupted American education and abridged vocabulary, could never impress or express.

Given a second chance, the school eventually placed me in third grade, where I hoped to belong. But there was a phrase that repeated in my head that being relegated or dethroned is twice as painful as any other struggle. Because losing something you thought was so deeply integrated into your identity is like mourning dreams curtailed. And so, I sat in the plastic blue chair, freezing under the air conditioner on a day at least 110 degrees; all feelings of hypocrisy and irony twisted and inextricably churned into glassy eyes. Like I dropped my books down the deep end. Undeniable, incriminating evidence on hands.

I started picking up nonfiction books, only because they appeared shorter and more manageable than the other fiction novellas that my peers traversed. The thinner the pages, the larger the print, the shorter the list of vocabulary words, I lingered around the crate to find the perfect short book. I gave my first book, a *National Geographic Kids* about amethysts, a light shuffle. And the more my classmates tried to find books that interested them, unknowingly taking on moral challenges and imaginative odysseys, I resorted to hard science—until my teacher finally approached me to question whether I'd actually read the book in five minutes. The sapphire or amethyst or whatever precious stone on the cover of the thin National Geographic book dulled into some shade of vinyl as I forgot how to explain what I'd read. Even though I wanted to tell her to know that I read, to let me read without being perceived, to leave me alone because whatever she thought of how fast I read or what questionable book choices I made would never change the way my life would turn out. I gave up on trying to explain myself; again, my words would never suffice.

She told me that I could "give up" a book and choose a new one, but I couldn't list a book on my list when I didn't *completely* read it. I'll never remember if I did *completely* finish the book, as someone ever defined what it meant to read a book *completely*: did I have to understand all the science behind how amethysts were made, when there were words in the book that I didn't understand but felt too intimidated to ask of my teachers? Did I have to memorize all the content or learn all the places that geodes were classified as amethysts by heart? Was I supposed to know this book beyond a frustrating feeling?

The Western narrative about how every problem could be quickly fixed with ease so gradually imposed throughout my early childhood soon turned its back on me, and the second I was away from Korea, I felt so utterly Korean against my will. I wish my teacher knew that being alone and mourning the time I lost my confidence in English weren't things I could fix on a random Tuesday. I can't just sit down on the "buddy bench" when I was trying to look like I was fine on my own. I can't just ask to sit with the large group of American girls when the entire class knew I only hung out with Korean children outside of class. I can't just tell my parents that their daughter is a pathetic third grader who averts challenges, fully knowing they would make her acknowledge some tongue-biting truth.

Recess became a time where I wandered around the corner of flat red shale, drawing faces on the rocks that looked too big with the rocks that looked too small, wishing I was with friends from my *Korean* church, eating *Korean* snacks, tucked in a cultural enclave instead of an overwhelming melting pot that made me insecure for being unamerican. Let me gauge out the guilt whenever I speak Korean from my bulging esophagus. I felt unnatural, unlike myself, but who was I supposed to be anymore? I was stuck in the pile of stones, like an uncut geode, answers to all the English questions unopened, books left as titles, friends into strangers, future unripe, faltering and in hiding.

The three months where I barely had friends may look like a choice to you, but you don't know all the times I mumbled words I forgot how to pronounce or deliberately walked away from conversations about American history or meticulously planned which book to read so my lack of confidence would never be exposed by anyone, again, ever. I'm sorry if all this looks like a choice to you.

For the first time, I understood the seemingly overrated concept of han, the intense emotions like fear, desperation, guilt, exhaustion, and the frustration that streamed from Korean folk tales. Blunt irony in the place where the practical stories of my childhood morphed into tragedies of insensitivity; it was exclusive in all the wrong places and inclusive in a way I didn't understand.

But what I didn't know in third grade was that becoming friends with one girl who was natural and confident yet not American broke every unspoken rule I'd abided by. Because she fit in regardless of her flag that embellished orange tones but no iconic red, white, or blue during a cultural activity, when my A4 sized Korean flag had all and only the colors of an American flag; she honed in on conversations about Houston and brands of color pencils from Michaels and which cereal had the best mini marshmallows from Target, when I tried to muster the most American answer I could give; she didn't care whether they misunderstood her or not and proclaimed every opinion she had like she was an abstract painting. Like they could judge and interpret her however they wanted, but she would still hold the inherent, objective meaning she thrust into her words; like she was internally untethered, a sapphire core untainted by erosion or weathering. Despite the six years I lived in Illinois and New Jersey, she was the one who appeared the most American, without knowing where either were on the map of the United States.

I now know that *han* isn't the full story of the war-ridden Koreans, because han is part of a complete arc of our people who embark on a journey to find *shinmyeong*, a state where we overcome the extenuating external circumstances to regain control of our lives. *Heung* decorates the arduous path to shinmyeong. Heung is the joy, the small celebrations that we enjoy, like Pringles and cookie M&Ms from rest stops amidst the ten-hour road trip. *Heung* is learning how to trust and love the process; heung is what keeps us going. To me, *heung* is the missing puzzle piece—the closure of miserable Korean folk tales. It is what helped me unite the dichotomy to a whole identity, because Western compliments of even incremental progress and *heung* are equivalent in my mind. It is *heung* that I found in the rocky friendships of playground or in the cafeteria or in my bedroom at 3 AM or even as I took the bus this morning.

I want to tell myself that it gets better. It is hard to believe, but childhood fears and nightmares flit anyways, and it doesn't matter what people think about me when I'll never see them in ten years. For so much of my life I've refused to let myself make mistakes, prescribed myself with insecurities, scrambled to fix them, desperately and meticulously, concealed all the times I've felt like an uncontrollable force changed the trajectory of my dreams, and often forgot that inside the seventeen year old trying to pursue chemistry lies a five year old who dreamed of becoming a notable author and artist, soaring into the blissful unknown, untethered and carefree. I want to tell myself to just let go.

The amethysts that I thought were stuck inside stones skept across water and floated along streams, weathered from storms and landslides, transient and adaptable and accepting of their smallness in the scheme of the world. A grain of corn in wild Illinois, short-lived dandelion seed, so be it, I'll join the force of nature, a sheen rock in the river until the geode cracks open for the world to see—yet a crystal is a crystal no matter how it's judged. I thank God every day that hard science exists, that people have found methodical ways to understand each other in a world of chaos. In my head, no matter what sort of crystal there exists, science will categorize and prove, and the people will judge or love, but the crystal will still exist in its entirety. I've learned that Koreans and Americans, to the best of their ability, try to take life with "a grain of salt" or "trust the process" or believe that every hardship comes with heung. Heung heals and lets me find peace, looking for my answers instead of the right ones.

I read most of the fiction books in the third row of shelves in my elementary school library. I improved my pronunciation when I stopped caring and started engaging. I put down the fear of how every sentence needs to be planned, perfect and pristine; I had two birthday parties for my American classmates and my Korean church friends. I learned to choose thicker books. I started competitive debate, partly because I needed to overcome my fear of public speaking, and partly to stay curious about the world. I switched so many friends in sixth grade; I accepted that I'll never learn the entirety of Korean dynasties but now know all the American presidents after AP US History. I overcame my fear of math through consistent practice and now I find it relaxing when improper integration falls into place and the series converges. I want to explore engineering after learning about solution architects. I want to be an artist and an author and a scientist and a daughter and an executive and a neighbor. I yearn for possibility in of itself; I'll burn out not like a fading star but as a supernova. I want to acknowledge that I am young and allowed to dream. I will challenge myself, and that I don't care whether they understand me or not. I don't care if they understand anyone at all. I will appreciate them if they try; I want to talk to people who do. In heung, I want to celebrate and be celebrated, untethered and free.

Korea is Abridged

Verbiage erupts when my pen pokes holes in the paper. Tiny black voids, empty and fruitless, lying dead like the dullness that resides in my damp words. I anchor you in holes—carved and unfulfilled, part of an indefinite whole. An expanse trails behind lost potential...An ellipsis because I omitted words to turn the silence into a pause, to fill void with purpose.

It was twelve when the tires hit the freeway. Twelve fifteen when we passed K-town and the small kimbap stand and July ice cream parlor and the bodega. I-95 and two half breaths out of drowsy suburbia. A cross on the dash, cross-legged shotgun, crossroad approaching my left eye—a bird shoots at the sun. Twelve thirty and you turn up the radio. The lyrics tangle in your silver hoops; I pull them out anyway for recalcitrant silence. Twelve fifty-two and you pull over two-thirds into the G.W. bridge with hair across shoulder and gaze affixed on mauve skyline. sober and sore and sunny in a slump and stretched across the wire, like the somber aftertaste of rain on a shore. Twelve fifty-nine and you hurtle your hoops into the Hudson because you listened after all. What calls from beneath?

What calls for the passenger seat? The sun tilts its reluctant head above the sunroof, and the rain escapes into a careless feeling. I stare—piercing through the lingering vastness of some unwanted nostalgia. I swerve past a corner like I'm in a race where no one wins, speeding through a swale of a road down Palisades Park, down the highway, perpetually chasing my front wheels because I feel I am behind. Crossed brow, crossed fervor, cross-armed backpack in the front seat, and lunchbox of soft seaweed and folds of ham sandwiches and animal crackers. I escape drowsy suburbia in a rush to feel a place more real, more withstanding against the glowering change that begins to unravel, benignly yet unknowingly, beneath the tattered leather of the steering wheel. The word vomit under pen now underpins the nausea that drives this car, 130 spirals per hour in tunnel vision. Gilt dies in tube. A bird shoots at the sun. Only when I pull over do I hear the reverberation of the radio. Twelve fifty-nine, and I miss you in the front seat. I miss the feeling of purple rice and ribbons of sesame oil and sweet radish in yuzu juice and honey crisp apples from upstate; I miss picking the giraffes out of my birthday cake flavored animal crackers and the vibrant jelly of persimmon like sweet summer on my tongue. I miss the lunch stuffed with crisp mandu and PB&J triangles sharp like origami corners. I miss when a starry feeling didn't remind me of its absence. I hurl what's left of my shimmer into the river. 1:03. I etch the time into rail and Manhattan outline into mind. Look through haze and fog wandering over water. Ponder what sinks under. The water is mud, ribbed, a desolate swamp and a prying calmness, a contrast to the speeding traffic whir.

When you took a left turn, the sparrow perched on the window fell into an abyss, the peach tree shivered in the dying November sun, wavering with a faint sugary note of summer, moms pulled their toddlers away from the wave of crushing traffic, and you hit the curb in a car that wasn't yours. A permit sticker sealed to the windowsill like a statement of youth and pen and paper mistakes. College-ruled loose leaf enclosed in a blanket of binders and wired in spiral notebooks; fresh paper encrusted with bejeweled September ambitions. You corked yourself in the small town that tucked you in an underwhelming youth, no possibility of a place greater than the dreams inside white picket fences.

A pigeon sits squat and prim on a viscid can. You toss your earrings into the river, in hopes that someone approaches you with at least a faint note of citrus and barley tea. The rot of sewage emerges from beneath like a rancid swarm of ungutted fish—encrusted in weed, I can tell. In the passenger seat, I watch you self-destruct into a form I've never seen before: tears hot and heavy down your face, covering the rearview mirror like a coward, wedging your glasses in the coffee-tainted cupholder–a keychain of *jagae* catches the light in your eye. You stuffed the mother-of-pearl into carved poppy petals and watched your mom skillfully smooth the thin film into corners, sliding yours into her palm, sorry and resentful that you didn't know what *jagae* meant in English and only knew *ughul*. You found Korea in *ughul*, the navy-like guilt that sank underneath your *bong soong ah,* balsam-stained, fingernails as you grasped a *kumdo* sword and noticed the softened carcasses unlike weathered leather patterned on your friends' palms. You saw ughul in the frustration and lost dreams of tying a black belt around your waist, when your friends forgot the belts in their closets because they moved on. You forced yourself to ignore your dream in the closet because you stayed. When you shared triangle *kimbap* with your childhood friends, you didn't have to clarify that the meal was a Korean rice ball, not Japanese onigiri, for the first time in nine years–but you didn't feel Korean at all.

Loneliness in America seeps through hardwood floors like a leak from a hurricane that never ends. It speaks in severed connections and deleted KakaoTalk group chats and the fear that I'll never be able to explain ughul, the feeling in-between frustration, sorrow, and grief to anyone. It is quiet and comforting when I watch my mom turn on K-drama compilations and bring home Korean groceries because *pah* is different from American green onions and shallots. It is the church retreats of Korean youth groups that unite in teenage versions of cultural enclaves. Loneliness in America resides in fruits I once neglected like *hanlabong*, a citrus native to the Korean island Jeju-do. I cling to the orange I bought at the farmer's market and trace an imaginary pear-like outline to create a *hanlabong* inside my mind; I bite into sour flesh. I retrace the hubbub and snacks made of love and *jungseong* (gift from the heart) of the *ohiljang* (five-day market) in the city view of the meatpacking district and Chelsea market's seafood corner. I miss the cheap *hanlabong* chocolate I picked with haste at the Jeju airport and its bittersweet aftertaste—a glimpse of community wrapped in artificial flavor.

I wonder if anyone would try traditional *hotteok* (chewy honey pancakes) from a street stand when all the K-town restaurants traded the chewy, tender, succulent pocket of syrup and smashed walnuts for a brittle circle with a taste of toasted flour, because in America, chewiness is often overcooked and undesirable. I know Koreans love tradition, but also the sacrifices of dedication. I see the guilt they feel for how they've scarred tradition for acceptance. In a heartbeat, they would buy *hotteok* as Koreans, not Korean-Americans. But in America, I am not the only one who feels alone, because no old ladies at the Grand Central Station see Korean-Americans as selfish people who left their country, escaping the weight of reconstruction. And so, I stand above the Hudson, orange in hand, knowing I will always swallow the brittle *hotteok* instead of the tender delicacy. In America, I am not a traitor, but a daughter, friend, and a part of a whole.

From the passenger seat, I watch you, myself if I never left America. You lean forward with your nose driven into the top of the steering wheel and rediscover old memories to place on the countertop. To remind yourself of what and why you left behind—a place you admired so much you had to leave before it broke you into glass shards. You buckle your seatbelt like a harness meant to keep you in place, from a dream sinking under, from thinking what if, from wondering if you were created for much else. Can you see right through me? Korea is the saying 웃을때 떠나라 (leave when they're smiling) because you left when everything could crystallize into pristine memories: a visit to the *ohiljang* in Jeju-do whenever you wanted to because you had a life to be lived. On the dash, the green digital time flashes to 3:01—you stare into the open river. You try to think about how the Hudson resembles the Hangang River, how Central Park is the *sumokwon* beneath your apartment complex, crossing your eyes to see the fine lines blur between the white pine and ginkgo leaves.

A lunchbox sits in the passenger seat. This morning, Umma helped me fill it with hand-picked giraffes from animal crackers, assorted berries from our garden, crispy mandu, and fresh yuzu radish. I wanted to ask her if I was the daughter she imagined her little girl, picking at the floral patterns on the *damyo* (summer blanket) and whispering, 어머나 세상에, 엄마한테 예쁜 제비꽃이 피었어요! I wanted to tell her that I still think pretty violets bloom on her blankets and dress and that they also grow from the crack in the sidewalk where *ughul* hides to haunt the future that never lasted.

America is the averted gaze, the escape from the life I could have lived.

Sargent and Woolf

I feel like I'm perpetually trapped in an abyss, a limbo state of being. I dread what will come, but I regret what has gone by. Maybe I've read too much Virginia Woolf.

I really shouldn't say this, but what's not to be said on my own blog? *To the Lighthouse* struck me. Gave me a bit of perspective on how time just exudes and seeps through my fingers. I need to fix my habit of noticing the "wrong" details in literature, but isn't literature subjective? Don't I hold the freedom to favor some interpretations of art over others? After all, my words, out of everything I can produce, possess most potency. The choice to read, to overanalyze in my own time empowers and acknowledges the futility of life and the allure of hedonism in a way that supports growth. In this post, I'll introduce the fragments that I like, the ones that everyone overlooks.

I love to be alone. No, I'm not a recluse. I don't like to be alone all the time, but the time that I spend with myself reassures me. "To be silent; to be alone. All the being and the doing, expansive, glittering, vocal, evaporated; and one shrunk, with a sense of solemnity, to being oneself, a wedge-shaped core of darkness, something invisible to others." I appreciate Woolf's vocabulary: "glittering" and "evaporated" just intuitively share the same sentiment of solemnity. I love the use of these words, because Woolf captures how imaginative contemplations, although pointless, futile, and hedonistic, can feed the soul. And it's also what a lot of people don't have the time for. Mrs. Ramsay barely has time for herself as a mother of eight, but when she does, she doesn't need to spend time looking within; she can look outwards, towards the flaws and soundness of her home, friends, and children. Being alone feels synonymous to standing in the corner of a party, people-watching, letting time, time that usually penetrates and crushes, soothe you for the first time. Lingering and being idle and stagnant inherently gratifies.

It gives me perspective. When you see the world from the window of a plane, even monolithic New York City appears miniscule. It feels futile… and Mrs. Ramsay shared this sentiment: "There were eternal problems: suffering, death, the poor…And yet she had said to all these children, You shall go through with it." Is she right in telling her children that they will endure? I don't know if I'm right in any aspect of life, yet art feels the same way. Am I using the right colors? Am I analyzing this right? What if this is just a mishap that I'm analyzing, just like the mistakes I make when I paint and write? I've seen many of Sargent's paintings lately. I love his brushstrokes, his ability to convey the natural landscapes of the world, such as the lofty peaks of the Canadian Rockies, along with the beauty of human life. I wonder how much time he was allowed to linger, to observe, to sit and be at peace with being idle for the pure pursuit of art. I wonder if I could ever do that, as an artist and writer. Maybe that's how he found certainty in his creative identity.

I feel anxious when I'm at rest. That sounds like a paradox, yet I feel more anxious when I'm not doing anything at all. And when Mrs. Ramsay has a second to spare, she catches a glimpse of all that could go wrong: "The light in the garden told her that; and the whitening of the flowers and something grey in the leaves conspired together to rouse in her a feeling of anxiety." There is something intuitive about gut-feelings or the way that Woolf writes this sentence. I'm unsure what is is, but the feeling that walls will curve inwards, the fear that stones will tumble down your esophagus, and the fear that you know that something is wrong, but you'll never be able to do anything about it, or that it happened completely in your control, will always frighten me.

Short Stories

Eight Summers Ago

"Did you close the windows near the laundry?" Umma[1] asks.

My contemplations wash away when I realize a fatal error in my *jangma*[2] preparation: I forgot to close the outer layer of the intricate Korean windows. When I enter the living room to lock the larger windows, the floor is already a gushing river. Rainwater soaks the fresh laundry I had just hung up on the dryer, submerges my favorite cotton slippers, and drowns my cacti. I hurl myself against the wind and wrap my arms around my clothes, tucking them safely underneath towels. When the window finally clicks into the latch, I dread turning around. Umma tells me to act with *nunchi* - read the room.

I look at the mess I have created. The rain has birthed giant puddles on the cherry wood floor that no longer boasts its gleaming brown polish, and the water reflects a decade's worth of chipped paint. Through the puddles, I spot a reflection of myself, revealing my distorted face in the murky water. In hindsight, because I dismissed Halmoni's[3] rules for her cherished floor and furniture, I know I'm the decade-long culprit of the excessive wear-and-tear, so I dig my nails into the heels of my palms as I remember every time that I had recklessly played tag or furiously swept on Halmoni's most prized possession. I rush to the kitchen before every memory cascades onto the ground and pools together in a muddy puddle of guilt and regret, infinitely expanding like the universe laughing back at me.

I grab a frail, ripped rag and desperately pat my mess. My mom calls me pathetic, and I grit my teeth in acceptance. I watch as the rainwater seeps between the cracks in the hardwood floor inside a room that I refuse to claim as mine. Maybe Halmoni treasured the floor because Korean floors are so intricate, designed to be kept cool during the summer and warmer during the winter. She used to lay the *yo*, or the mattress, on the ground and tuck me in my blanket woven with vibrant florals and embroidered with techniques passed down in my lineage for centuries– until my birth. In the heavens, my ancestors probably wallow in grief that their family traditions, so intricate and glittering and worth being shared and celebrated with the world, have been butchered by their clumsy, callow teenage descendant: a true case of involuntary manslaughter. My soggy fingertips sting from the holes I've punctured in my skin instead of the fabric. I wonder if Halmoni will ever forgive me for neglecting her embroidery and polished floor, and for yearning to leave this house to escape from the perennial evidence of my petty crimes. I plug in Halmoni's old hair dryer to the nearest outlet and let the warm air blow at the ground until some of the puddle evaporates. Although the water on my hands dries, my stubborn guilt will never evaporate.

The floor is not completely dry yet and looks like a mosaic of old, yellowed rags, but I move on to my slippers. Drying them with Halmoni's hair dryer, I regret that I peered outside, drumming my fingers to the chirping tunes of the cicada flocks on the birch instead of listening to her. My mother's family never had a dialect, and yet the Korean language still traveled in monotone fleets, swimming between the pitches and inflections of the English tones that I understood, perpetually stuck in the vacant space between the Anglican treble and bass clef notes. After five years of piano lessons, I felt like I had an unfortunate, peculiar abnormality of two left hands and music note dyslexia, and I couldn't bear to decipher the furious annotations on my music sheets or the connotations behind the Korean language. How could I understand or play the same tune if I couldn't tell which fingers should press the keys?

"Don't wear these outside the house, okay?" Halmoni said when she first handed me the soft slippers eight summers ago. The same week, I carelessly wore them outside to a *bingsoo* store with her and Haraboji.[4] I grabbed my grandparents' hands and obliviously ate the frozen dessert, unaware of why my grandmother suggested going outside when I asked about her absence every Wednesday. I dug through flakes of ice, ravaging the decadent rice cakes and red bean paste, in search of everything but the truth. The raindrops drip off the slippers and onto the ground, creating another puddle. *Is this actually working?*

I walk into the dimly lit bathroom, holding my cacti, and pour out water into the sink. The leaves droop and fall off the sickly and almost dead stem, and soggy spines bend against my fingers. Although I don't bleed, I would rather be pierced by adamant thorns instead of sad pricks. Cacti evolved spines as a survival mechanism to prevent water loss in arid deserts at the expense of losing their ability to withstand floods. Cacti are supposed to be low maintenance, to be taken care of with ease, and yet, I had ravaged a succulent pot of this thriving living organism. However, Halmoni's favorite small fuchsia-shade flowers on the tips of the branches are still alive and in full bloom. My spine curls over the sink, watching the flowers sag, sitting in giant puddles of futility in the vase. When the plant dies, the flowers will wilt as well.

Eight *jangmas* ago, no one was inside Halmoni's house when the sun filled the room with its radiant morning light and gushed into my vision. I secretly listened to Umma's call with Haraboji when she returned home hours later. As tears rolled down my cheeks, I sat in silence until they became choking sobs. My fingers locked into each other and around my mouth like a tight clasp until I choked back words that never existed. The rain should have poured in buckets from the heavens, the air should have suffocated and crushed with overbearing humidity, the atmosphere should have erupted from the storms it was holding, and the sun should have refused to shine. Yet, the sun beamed in the blue sky and I heard laughter from the neighborhood playground; it was just another beautiful day for everyone outside Halmoni's house.

As I walk back into the room, sunlight pours through the windows, drying the rag-covered floors and slippers while I drown in grief. Eight summers have passed, but I am still alone in the shadows of my grandmother. The sunlight has not reached me yet.

Everlasting June

Your guts don't feel like they're falling apart. Some feel like they've turned into the heaviest rocks, the hardest, roughest, jagged, and serrated river bedrocks, eroded by the currents inside you that flow in all the different directions you could ever imagine, and some others, the skipping stones, bloat and float upwards and skim up your esophagus; they once said that you could drown from the inside as your lungs fill up with mucus, but I believe this way of drowning still comes second to the rocks.

Do the rocks appear when you lose hope? June and I once climbed up the mountain behind our school. We hiked through the muddy pathways, the colossal trees, and the streams, all full of life, until we stood under a cliff. As June scaled the edge of the rocks, I watched her disappear into the clouds above; rising, she was gone. Below, for hours, I waited for her to return. As our friends searched for us, the rescue team arrived, and June's parents and teachers mourned her disappearance. I couldn't stop myself from believing in her, whispering to myself that she would come back. And she did.

Just wait and see. Naïveté is your deadliest sin, and having hope and faith will devastate you. But what happens in the absence of innocence? I've lost naïveté, my foolish, callow habits of impatiently awaiting the future. I no longer feel the swaying of the skipping stones bottled in my throat because the stones have settled and stacked up into neat towers. Koreans believe pebble towers make your wishes come true, but I feel like all my pebbles fail to bring prosperity, or even plain luck. Now, I'm standing under my too tall wishing tower, a skyscraper of deferred dreams, wishing that it won't tip over and smite me in a thousand different places, a thousand in cacophony.

June and I hope all the time. When we sprint across the field of daisies behind the playground, when we braid dandelions into our hair, when we share popsicles and lemonade, we share dreams, dreams that fall gently like the ice cream dribbling down our chins.

What if I feel like I was stripped of my dreams? I couldn't control what happened, and so I chose to reject and despair alone, all because I lacked guts, and shambles of rueful stones sat where my resilience once stood. I entombed myself under my blankets; I closed my eyes and prepared to cross the river Styx; alas, light seeped through my eyelids, and when I awakened, I counted all the crumbs on the popcorn ceiling above my bed. I never realized that days could feel like months until I resided in a prison, rotting behind bars I built for myself. It was so quiet inside that I couldn't breathe, even when I needed to break the silence.

What happened? I love being outside. Everything you're saying is scaring me.

Do you want to know? I knew since I was nine years old. Before the ninth Christmas of my life, in the frigid breeze on the ice rink, June laid askew, scarlet clots lined her lips. Her eyes - once perceptive and daring - stared in a vacuous glance at the falling snow; her arms sprawled and grasped for something she could no longer yearn for. I stood above her bellying pool of blood like a deer in headlights, a helpless damsel in distress, and I clutched the fur of my jacket more tightly than I could ever hold her lifeless body that emanated a still, nightmarish lightness. I ran as far as I could.

I wish I had turned back, watched her longer, and questioned if her aloof expression signified her fall into limbo between heaven and hell, or heaven and Earth. Doctors at the emergency room whispered in soft hushes, their hands coalescing with those of June's parents. Their cheekbones wilted and sagged onto the tiles of the sterile floor.

My parents put on a disguise of deceit that December, covered in red pajamas and eating the cookies I had left behind. Dim incandescence; muted gilt. Sunken below drapes of tinsel and curls of mistletoe wreath, I was the only child sulking in bed; my parents waltzed in and pulled me out into the living room. Eyes radiant in the sun's dawn luster, I stumbled towards the tree. On the hem of the tree skirt laid presents, wrapped in the shiniest packaging and satin ribbons and a single envelope that glistened. I felt rewarded. I was glorious and triumphant and beloved, all just for living through another year. For I had thought that this one Christmas, I could savor my presents, taking life for granted, just like how I once believed in a tomorrow that was promised.

I gingerly opened the envelope and read. "You've been such a good child this year. You've been kind to your parents and caring to the people around you. I want to thank you for growing up to become a sweet child." Those lines picked at the scabs I wished I could ignore. Because I knew, I noticed my parents had written this letter and that there was no man named Santa Claus. In fact, there was no such person who could or wanted to understand what had happened. If anyone knew, if my parents knew, and if an omniscient magical figure like Santa Claus knew, they wouldn't have called me a "sweet child." I felt the paper pry my cuts open, shoving skipping stones through my flesh and into my throat. What sweet child runs from her dying best friend?

The climax is not death but its acceptance. The worst part of drowning is not feeling your lungs, your flesh, and your veins fill up with water. It's when you realize how bad it's going to feel as you dissolve. Death is not fleeting. Death is long in the moment because pain and agony and rejection take an eternity to process. No book can record your death. Death writes your pages in your head, in your body, and in your heart, and you see yourself slowly becoming absorbed by this sensation. You don't feel death all at once; you feel death encroaching upon you. And it's not one of those horror movie scenes in which a character suddenly dies after a lurking figure towers overhead. It's those recurring daily events and episodes where you know you can feel that it's going to be the end. It's the change and shift you can feel in between all the faces you make. It's the beginning of the movie where the protagonist finds a rising action that leads to the climax: embracing death. There is no alternative in which the main character overcomes death. And the worst metaphor of it all is that "they slip away into darkness," and it's the worst not only because it's overused, but also because it's true. You can tell when someone begins to fade and lets go of everything they once had. You can tell it in their face and in their minds and everything about them shows that they've reached the climax. They've reached their limit in both life and the process of dying.

My naïveté is a burden proved, and its weight will fall on your shoulders like guilt inherited. I wish you wouldn't have to grow into the shadow I became, yet I know you would choose all the same tortuous paths because I was once you. While both of us await an everlasting June, her death froze the seasons countless Decembers ago.

Behind Barriers

I: Inside

The foreign embassies in Delhi trapped their ambassadors behind their tall, resilient brick walls, some even topped with thick metal fences or spikes of barbed wire. Luxurious hotels and malls across India required a stringent identification process to enter. My school, the American Embassy School, surrounded all corners of their campus with maximum security and armed police.

Through the twelve feet tall, stained gates, and then through a concealed door, I arrived at school every day. Ever since I had departed from Korea, I grew accustomed to these unusual daily routines. I began shoveling the granular, sandy part of the playground with my shoes, reminiscent of digging my boots through the friendly, soft snow. The early morning fog dissipated to unveil the sun that approached dangerously close to the playground, relentlessly parching everything under its rays.

That particular morning, I filled in paper cutouts of peace signs, sliding my color pencil that left only a light lavender mark while my classmates aggressively scrubbed their papers with the brittle graphite. Tedious yet easy work about global harmony, generosity, and altruism marked the beginning of the sunny October school days, followed by consecutive lessons about the global community. My school bestowed this assignment with the aspirational name, "Peace Project," and that day, we explored a video of International Peace Day. My classmates and I, citizens from many different countries, watched as the projector beamed a video of an activist dedicating an entire day for international reconciliation; we were unified at school.

From the third floor of the elementary school building, all we could see was the rest of the spacious campus below us that ended at the tall walls. An adamant stone barrier, barricading the rest of the city from us, stood resolutely to create an enclosure. In third grade, the age "nine" sounded rhythmic to our ears, deceiving us that a decade of life experience sufficed, yet only a letter away from the term, "none;" our ingenuous minds allowed these acres of four-story terracotta brick buildings to encompass our entire worlds. Staying within our school grounds erased cultural boundaries, even the traces of endemic Indian details.

The stone table was covered with containers of unique, cultural meals, overflowing with Greek baklava, Korean tteokbokki, and the cliché ham and cheese sandwiches; their scents permeated the lunch bags and the surrounding air. Despite the enticing sight of vibrant lunch boxes, the playground appealed to us the most. When we played tag in this weather, drops of sweat dribbled down our cheeks, pollution filled our lungs with every breath, and copious amounts of water plunged down our throats. I picked up my pace to venture through the colossal Banyan tree's limp roots that collapsed like drapes of sheer curtains, stretching laterally across the playground. One, two, three, four - I entered the soccer field past the fourth branch where my friends were resting on the grass. This particular recess, a tiresome, humid haze of silence rested above us.

"Why did they build these walls?" I inquired, shattering the silence.

"To protect us," my friend Maris said, watching the sky as she ran her fingers through the scorching artificial grass on the school field.

"From what?" Could they possibly be afraid of the monkeys, stray dogs, or peacocks in the city? Trapped inside tall fences, frightened of the wild animals outside their cages, our school put irony on display.

As her eyes reflected the dark clouds, Maris whispered, "To protect us from the people outside. We can't be the same as them." Immediately, from her jacket pocket, she pulled out a piece of caramel and vigorously chewed, spreading the buttery sweetness all around her mouth as if to cleanse the aftertaste of her bitter words.

I lifted my palms from the superficial grass and stopped staring at the clouds like a pet parrot that obediently repeated what its owner wished it to say, all in the hopes of leaving its cage. Some of the plastic blades of grass ripped from the rubber ground and remained between my sweaty fingers like my nauseous guilt. I longed to justify these walls, to realize they didn't resemble an enclosure, and to believe that my friends didn't separate themselves, patronizing with a smug sense of superiority, from the Indian public.

Cold air brushed the sweat across my forehead as I ecstatically pulled the door open, leaving sandy footprints on the steps of the school bus. When I walked through the aisle, a piercing cool breeze punctured me, and when I sat down in my seat, I shivered from the air conditioning. My embarrassment bloomed into the largest pink peonies on my face when I glanced outside at the people on the rickshaws, driving through the heatwaves and staring at the overbearing walls of my school as security guards opened its bothersome metal exit. When I left the "inside," I picked the flowers off my face and stuffed them into my pockets. I spilled them regardless when my pockets finally ripped from the harrowing guilt that gathered into neat piles of bloody petals.

II: To create a mirage

Blood trickled down my lip as I bit into the soft flesh inside my mouth. Standing on the balcony of my apartment building, my bulky mask with several plastic air filters clung, webbed and sewn through the corners of my lips. My lungs, barren from asthma, ached from the air pollution that congested the night sky; I peered at the moon's blurry halo of light, squinting in hopes that my poor eyesight muted it instead of fossil fuels. Wearily staring at the horizon strangely cured the insomnia clouding my mind.

Within three years, I watched rusty construction vehicles crowd the sandy landscape with lofty skyscrapers, too high for anyone to reach. However, people somehow filled the buildings to their brims and turned on bright lights on every floor. Walking on the streets beside these towering structures, I squinted as the gleams that bounced off their corners and blinded pedestrians, refusing to let me glance at their ceilings. As I gazed above from a tall apartment balcony, they reluctantly allowed me to carefully peek at their tops. What were they hiding? Nothing peculiar, except rooftop havens of iridescence, slim palm trees, and vibrant orchids, residents flocked to soft burgundy carpets, even when sandstorms filled the lungs of everyone below.

Groups of tents, makeshift portable canvas shelters decked with frail wood planks and tattered, crimson-stained paisley rugs sat askew. The orchid petals fell, enveloped the paisley teardrop patterns, symbolic of life and fertility, yet no longer visible underneath the profligacy. The glass panels that adorned the extravagant buildings reflected light everywhere but cast shadows on these homes. During the summer, the buildings provided shade for the families living underneath the piles of rugs, but they showed little mercy for them in India's winters.

A security guard shooed, whipped stray dogs and pigs from the entrance of my apartment. I snatched my mask off my face and rubbed the blood-soaked mask under running water, but the stains resisted. Exhausted, waiting for guidance, advice, or selfish encouragement, I silently observed these struggles from the comfort of my air-conditioned room; I embraced naïveté.

In the cloudy sky, the constellations of stars that delivered sleep were a mirage, nothing more than superficial office lights. The hazy pollution masked everything, and I protected my lungs, but my eyes, blinded by the heat, no longer witnessed the truth.

III: Luster in the haze

The end decorated me with a floral vestige. My friends handed me vibrant marigold garlands, wrapped them around my neck like a medal, and let them go after a series of hugs. Inside my empty house, the flowers became the lone centerpiece trapped inside a large, silver vase. I stared at the aberrant petals, left behind as orange remnants of my childhood, until the last day of farewell.

My suitcase trailed behind me as I paced along the airport terminal, heading to my flight. Only five minutes until takeoff. I fidgeted with the loose, estranged threads dangling from my sleeves; the distinct vermilion threads resembled the alienated marigolds.

My seat was embroidered with gold henna designs. I picked at the fringe until the faint streetlights, bustling night markets, glistening apartment windows, and the rush hour traffic all fused into a single amber luster. Yet, my eyes and those of the passengers only reflected the skyscrapers that towered above the haze, above all life.

About the Author

Jiyoo Choi is a writer, artist, and scientist from Seoul, Korea. An aspiring chemist, Jiyoo bonds themes of identity, grief, and sense of self to speak with resonance. Her unique voice has earned recognition from the Scholastic Art & Writing Awards, Blue Marble Review, Creative Communications Poetry Contest, and more. As a competitive debater, Jiyoo has placed top 6th at the 49th Harvard National Forensics Tournament and 8th at the Thistle Cup. She lives to create—and for matcha.

www.ingramcontent.com/pod-product-compliance
Lightning Source LLC
Chambersburg PA
CBHW021933170626
46807CB00007B/3094